Rain, Rain, Go Away!

— a book of —
Nursery Rhymes

First published in the United States 1991 by
Dial Books for Young Readers
A Division of Penguin Books USA Inc.
375 Hudson Street · New York, New York 10014

Published in Great Britain by Collins Publishers
Copyright © 1990 by Jonathan Langley
All rights reserved
Printed in Great Britain
First Edition
E
1 3 5 7 9 10 8 6 4 2

Library of Congress Cataloging in Publication Data
Rain, rain, go away! a book of nursery rhymes
illustrated by Jonathan Langley.
p. cm.
Includes index.
Summary: A collection of nursery rhymes,
some of which are chants and games.
ISBN 0-8037-0762-2
1. Nursery rhymes. 2. Children's poetry.
[1. Nursery rhymes.] I. Langley, Jonathan, ill.
PZ8.3.R1445 1991 398.8—dc20 89-34594 CIP AC

Rain, Rain, Go Away!

—a book of—
Nursery Rhymes

Illustrated by Jonathan Langley

Dial Books for Young Readers
New York

CONTENTS

Let's Begin

Out goes the rat,
Out goes the cat,
Out goes the lady
With the big green hat.
Y, O, U, spells you;
O, U, T, spells out!

Eenie, meenie, minie, mo,
Catch a tiger by the toe,
If he hollers, let him go,
Eenie, meenie, minie, mo.

6

One potato, two potato,
Three potato, four;
Five potato, six potato,
Seven potato, MORE.

Dip dip dip,
My blue ship,
Sailing on the water,
Like a cup and saucer.
Dip dip dip,
You're not It.

Ickle ockle, blue bockle,
Fishes in the sea,
If you want a pretty maid,
Please choose me.

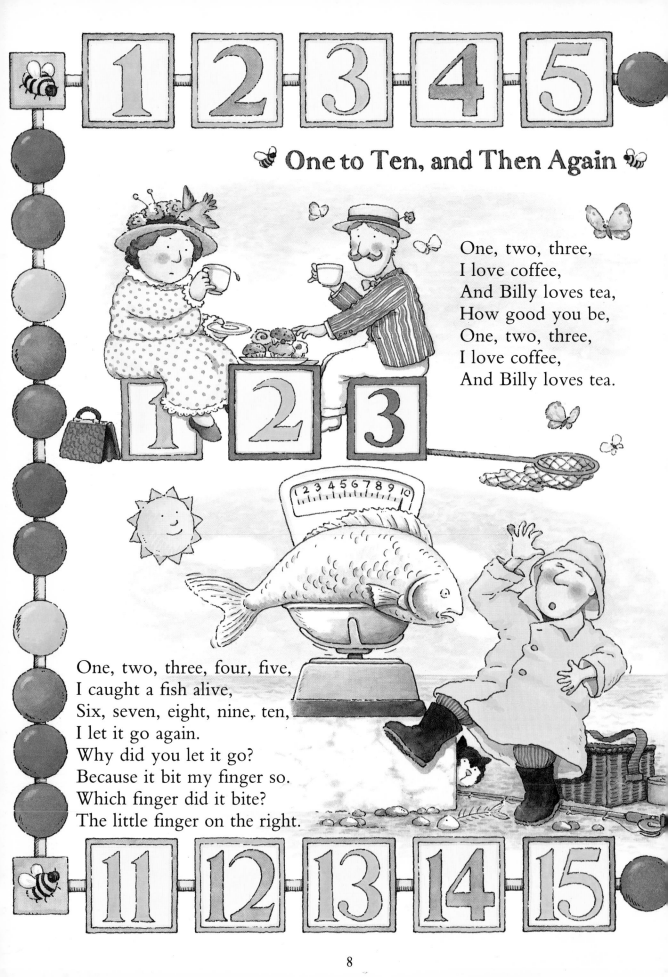

🐝 One to Ten, and Then Again 🐝

One, two, three,
I love coffee,
And Billy loves tea,
How good you be,
One, two, three,
I love coffee,
And Billy loves tea.

One, two, three, four, five,
I caught a fish alive,
Six, seven, eight, nine, ten,
I let it go again.
Why did you let it go?
Because it bit my finger so.
Which finger did it bite?
The little finger on the right.

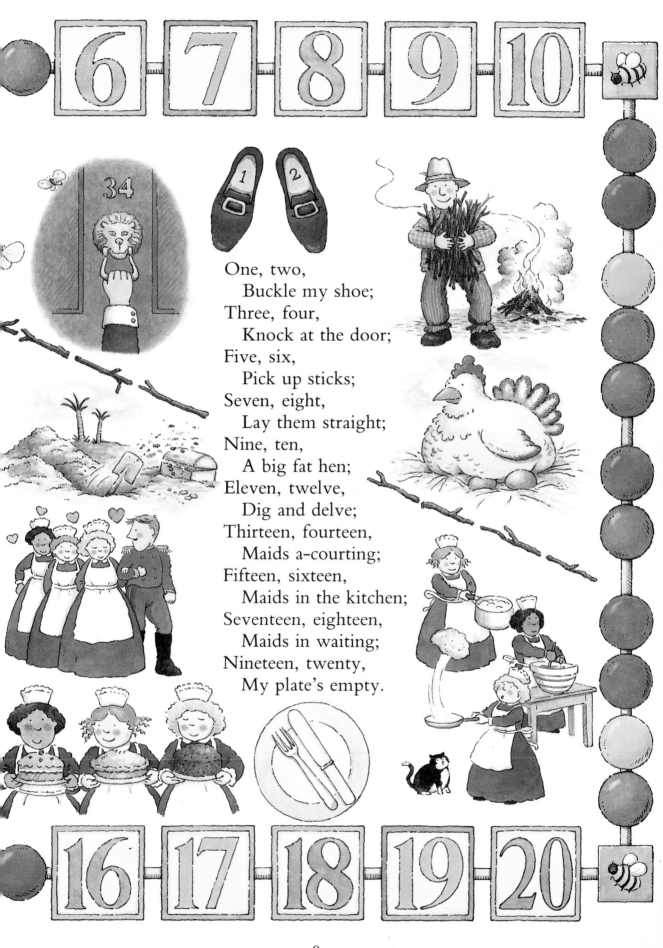

One, two,
  Buckle my shoe;
Three, four,
  Knock at the door;
Five, six,
  Pick up sticks;
Seven, eight,
  Lay them straight;
Nine, ten,
  A big fat hen;
Eleven, twelve,
  Dig and delve;
Thirteen, fourteen,
  Maids a-courting;
Fifteen, sixteen,
  Maids in the kitchen;
Seventeen, eighteen,
  Maids in waiting;
Nineteen, twenty,
  My plate's empty.

Nursery Days

Bye, baby bunting,
Daddy's gone a-hunting,
Gone to get a rabbit skin
To wrap the baby bunting in.

Pat-a-cake, pat-a-cake, baker's man,
Bake me a cake as fast as you can;
Pat it and prick it, and mark it with B,
Put it in the oven for Baby and me.

Dance to your daddy,
    My little babby,
Dance to your daddy,
    My little lamb.

You shall have a fishy
    In a little dishy,
You shall have a fishy
    When the boat comes in.

You shall have an apple,
    You shall have a plum,
You shall have a rattle
    When your daddy comes home.

Rock-a-bye, baby, on the treetop,
When the wind blows, the cradle will rock;
When the bough breaks, the cradle will fall,
And down will come baby, cradle and all.

How many days has my baby to play?
Saturday, Sunday, Monday,
Tuesday, Wednesday, Thursday, Friday,
Saturday, Sunday, Monday.
   Hop away, skip away,
   My baby wants to play;
My baby wants to play every day!

Baby Games

This little piggy went to market;
This little piggy stayed at home;
This little piggy had roast beef;
This little piggy had none;
This little piggy cried, Wee, wee, wee,
　　All the way home.

Tickly, tickly, on your knee,
If you laugh you don't love me.

Round and round the garden,
Goes the teddy bear;
One step, two step,
Tickle you under there!

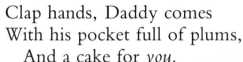

Clap hands, Daddy comes
With his pocket full of plums,
And a cake for *you*.

This is the way the ladies ride,
  Nim, nim, nim, nim.
This is the way the gentlemen ride,
  Trim, trim, trim, trim.
This is the way the farmers ride,
  Trot, trot, trot, trot.
This is the way the huntsmen ride,
  A-gallop, a-gallop, a-gallop, a-gallop.
This is the way the ploughboys ride,
  Hobble-de-hoy, hobble-de-hoy.

Here are the lady's knives and forks,
Here is the lady's table,
Here is the lady's looking glass,
And here is the baby's cradle.

I Love Little Pussy

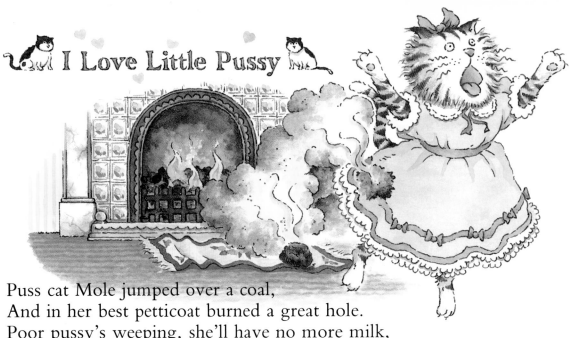

Puss cat Mole jumped over a coal,
And in her best petticoat burned a great hole.
Poor pussy's weeping, she'll have no more milk,
Until her best petticoat's mended with silk.

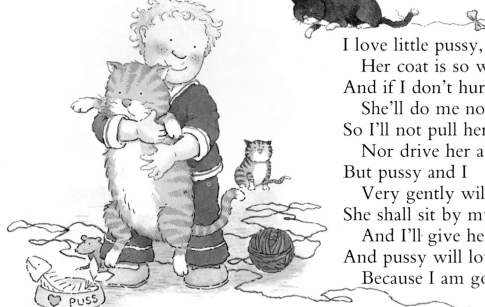

I love little pussy,
　Her coat is so warm,
And if I don't hurt her
　She'll do me no harm.
So I'll not pull her tail,
　Nor drive her away,
But pussy and I
　Very gently will play.
She shall sit by my side,
　And I'll give her some food;
And pussy will love me
　Because I am good.

Sing, sing,
　What shall I sing?
The cat's run away
　With the pudding string!
Do, do,
　What shall I do?
The cat's run away
　With the pudding too!

Pussy cat ate the dumplings,
Pussy cat ate the dumplings,
    Mamma stood by,
    And cried, Oh, fie!
Why did you eat the dumplings?

Who's that ringing at my door bell?
    A little pussy cat that isn't very well.
Rub its little nose with a little mutton fat,
    That's the best cure for a little pussy cat.

Ding, dong, bell,
Pussy's in the well.
Who put her in?
Little Johnny Green.
Who pulled her out?
Little Tommy Stout.
What a naughty boy was that
To try to drown poor pussy cat,
Who never did him any harm,
And killed the mice in his father's barn.

Mice Galore

Three blind mice, see how they run!
They all ran after the farmer's wife,
Who cut off their tails with a carving knife,
Did you ever see such a sight in your life,
    As three blind mice?

Three young rats with black felt hats,
Three young ducks with white straw flats,

Three young dogs with curling tails,
Three young cats with demi-veils,

Went out to walk with two young pigs
In satin vests and sorrel wigs;

But suddenly it chanced to rain
And so they all went home again.

Hickory, dickory, dock,
The mouse ran up the clock.
   The clock struck one,
   The mouse ran down,
Hickory, dickory, dock.

Six little mice sat down to spin;
Pussy passed by and she peeped in.
What are you doing, my little men?
Weaving coats for gentlemen.
Shall I come in and cut off your threads?
No, no, Mistress Pussy,
You'd bite off our heads.
Oh, no, I'll not; I'll help you to spin.
That may be so, but you can't come in.

Sing a Song of Sixpence

Sing a song of sixpence,
  A pocket full of rye;
Four and twenty blackbirds,
  Baked in a pie.

When the pie was opened,
  The birds began to sing;
Wasn't that a dainty dish,
  To set before the king?

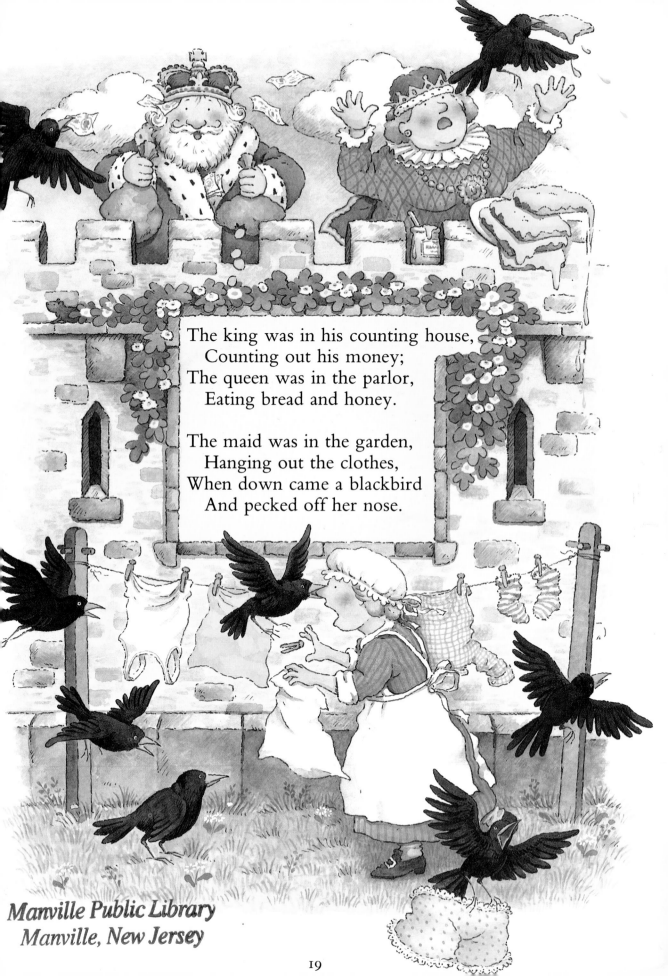

The king was in his counting house,
Counting out his money;
The queen was in the parlor,
Eating bread and honey.

The maid was in the garden,
Hanging out the clothes,
When down came a blackbird
And pecked off her nose.

Birds of the Air

A wise old owl sat in an oak,
The more he heard the less he spoke;
The less he spoke the more he heard.
Why aren't we all like that wise old bird?

Jenny Wren fell sick
Upon a merry time,
In came Robin Redbreast
And brought her soup and wine.

Eat well of the soup, Jenny,
Drink well of the wine.
Thank you, Robin, kindly,
You shall be mine.

Jenny Wren got well,
And stood upon her feet,
And told Robin plainly,
She loved him not a bit.

Robin he got angry,
And hopped upon a twig,
Saying, Out upon you, fie upon you,
Bold faced jig!

Little Poll Parrot
Sat in his garret
Eating toast and tea;
A little brown mouse
Jumped into the house,
And stole it all away.

Little Robin Redbreast
Came to visit me;
This is what he whistled,
Thank you for my tea.

Pit, pat, well-a-day,
Little Robin flew away.
Where can little Robin be?
Gone into the cherry tree.

There were two birds sat on a stone,
    Fa, la, la, la, lal, de;
One flew away, and then there was one,
    Fa, la, la, la, lal, de;
The other flew after, and then there was none,
    Fa, la, la, la, lal, de;
And so the poor stone was left all alone,
    Fa, la, la, la, lal, de.

I Saw a Ship a-Sailing

I saw a ship a-sailing,
A-sailing on the sea,
And oh, but it was laden
With pretty things for thee!

There were chocolates in the cabin,
And apples in the hold;
The sails were made of silk,
And the masts were all of gold.

The four-and-twenty sailors,
That stood between the decks,
Were four-and-twenty white mice
With chains about their necks.

The captain was a duck
With a packet on his back,
And when the ship began to move
The captain said, Quack! Quack!

The House that Jack Built

This is the house that Jack built.

This is the malt
That lay in the house
that Jack built.

This is the rat,
That ate the malt
That lay in the house
that Jack built.

This is the cat,
That killed the rat,
That ate the malt
That lay in the house
that Jack built.

This is the dog,
That worried the cat,
That killed the rat,
That ate the malt
That lay in the house
that Jack built.

This is the cow with the crumpled horn,
That tossed the dog,
That worried the cat,
That killed the rat,
That ate the malt
That lay in the house
that Jack built.

This is the maiden all forlorn,
That milked the cow with the crumpled horn,
That tossed the dog,
That worried the cat,
That killed the rat,
That ate the malt
That lay in the house
that Jack built.

This is the man all tattered and torn,
That kissed the maiden all forlorn,
That milked the cow
with the crumpled horn,
That tossed the dog,
That worried the cat,
That killed the rat,
That ate the malt
That lay in the house
that Jack built.

This is the priest all shaven and shorn,
That married the man all tattered and torn,
That kissed the maiden all forlorn,
That milked the cow with the crumpled horn,
That tossed the dog,
That worried the cat,
That killed the rat,
That ate the malt
That lay in the house
that Jack built.

This is the cock that crowed in the morn,
That waked the priest all shaven and shorn,
That married the man all tattered and torn,
That kissed the maiden all forlorn,
That milked the cow with the crumpled horn,
That tossed the dog,
That worried the cat,
That killed the rat,
That ate the malt
That lay in the house
that Jack built.

Nonsensical Rhymes

Hey diddle, diddle,
The cat and the fiddle,
The cow jumped over the moon;
The little dog laughed
To see such sport,
And the dish ran away with
    the spoon.

Hoddley, poddley, puddle and fogs,
Cats are to marry the poodle dogs;
Cats in blue jackets and dogs in red hats,
What will become of the mice and the rats?

Humpty Dumpty sat on a wall,
Humpty Dumpty had a great fall;
All the King's horses
And all the King's men
Couldn't put Humpty together again.

Rub-a-dub-dub,
Three men in a tub,
And how do you think they got there?
The butcher, the baker,
The candlestick maker,
They all jumped out of a rotten potato,
'Twas enough to make someone stare.

Owen Moore went away,
Owing more than he could pay.
Owen Moore came back next day,
Owing more.

A man in the wilderness, he asked me,
How many strawberries grow in the sea?
I answered him, as I thought good,
As many red herrings as swim in the wood.

Mother, may I go out to swim?
    Yes, my darling daughter.
Hang your clothes on a hickory limb
    And don't go near the water.

In the City, In the Street

London Bridge is falling down,
Falling down, falling down;
London Bridge is falling down,
My fair lady.

We must build it up again,
Up again, up again;
We must build it up again,
My fair lady.

All around the cobbler's bench,
The monkey chased the weasel;
That's the way the money goes,
   Pop goes the weasel!

A penny for a spool of thread,
A penny for a needle;
That's the way the money goes,
   Pop goes the weasel!

Every night when I go out,
The monkey's on the table;
Take a stick and knock it off,
   Pop goes the weasel!

Sally go round the sun,
Sally go round the moon,
Sally go round the chimney tops
On a Saturday afternoon.

Oranges and lemons,
　　Say the bells of St Clement's.
You owe me five farthings,
　　Say the bells of St Martin's.
When will you pay me?
　　Say the bells of Old Bailey.
When I grow rich,
　　Say the bells of Shoreditch.
When will that be?
　　Say the bells of Stepney.
I'm sure I don't know,
　　Says the Great Bell of Bow.

Mary had a little lamb,
　　Its fleece was white as snow;
And everywhere that Mary went
　　The lamb was sure to go.

It followed her to school one day,
　　That was against the rule;
It made the children laugh and play
　　To see a lamb at school.

dog
sheep

And so the teacher turned it out,
  But still it lingered near,
And waited patiently about
  Till Mary did appear.

Why does the lamb love Mary so?
  The eager children cry;
Why, Mary loves the lamb, you know,
  The teacher did reply.

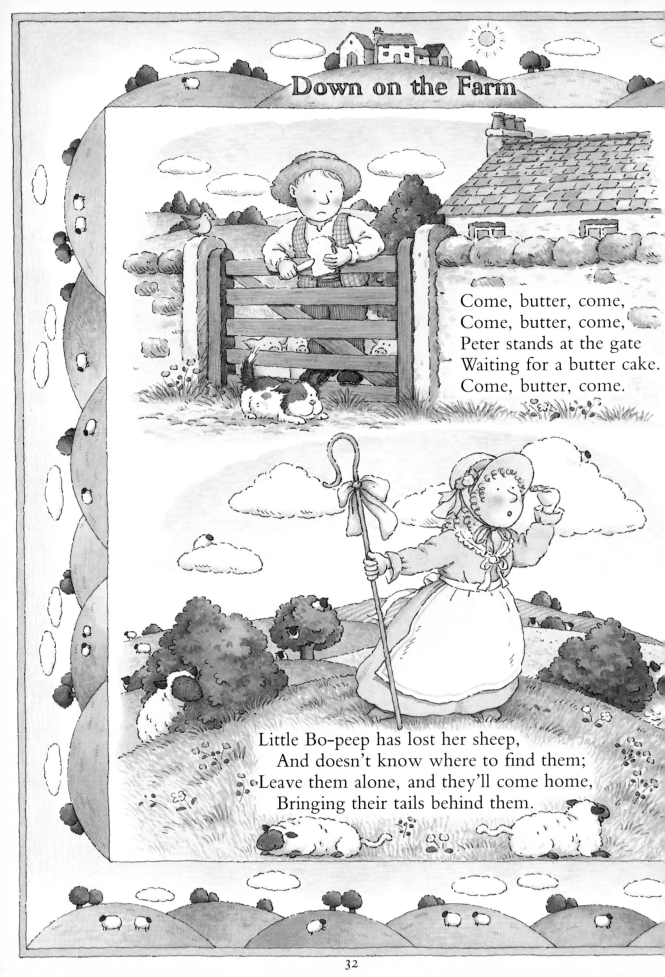

Down on the Farm

Come, butter, come,
Come, butter, come,
Peter stands at the gate
Waiting for a butter cake.
Come, butter, come.

Little Bo-peep has lost her sheep,
And doesn't know where to find them;
Leave them alone, and they'll come home,
Bringing their tails behind them.

If I had a donkey that wouldn't go,
Would I beat him? Oh no, no.
I'd put him in the barn and give him some corn,
The best little donkey that ever was born.

Baa, baa, black sheep,
　　Have you any wool?
Yes, sir, yes, sir,
　　Three bags full;
One for the master,
　　And one for the dame,
And one for the little boy
　　Who lives down the lane.

Yankee Doodle came to town,
Riding on a pony;
He stuck a feather in his cap
And called it macaroni.

I had a little pony,
His name was Dapple Gray;
I lent him to a lady
To ride a mile away.
She whipped him, she lashed him,
She rode him through the mire,
I would not lend my pony now,
For all the lady's hire.

Ride a cockhorse to Banbury Cross,
To see a fine lady upon a white horse;
Rings on her fingers and bells on her toes,
She shall have music wherever she goes.

Shoe a little horse,
Shoe a little mare,
But let the little colt
Go bare, bare, bare.

A farmer went trotting upon his grey mare,
 Bumpety, bumpety, bump!
With his daughter behind him so rosy and fair,
 Lumpety, lumpety, lump!

A raven cried, Croak! and they all tumbled down,
 Bumpety, bumpety, bump!
The mare broke her knees and the farmer his crown,
 Lumpety, lumpety, lump!

The mischievous raven flew laughing away,
 Bumpety, bumpety, bump!
And vowed he would serve them the same the next day,
 Lumpety, lumpety, lump!

Cherry Stone Rhymes

Who shall I marry?

Tinker,
Tailor,
Soldier,
Sailor,
Rich man,
Poor man,
Beggar man,
Thief.

When will it be?

This year,
Next year,
Sometime,
Never.

Where shall I marry?

Church,
Temple,
Cathedral,
Abbey.

And the ring?

Gold,
Silver,
Copper,
Brass.

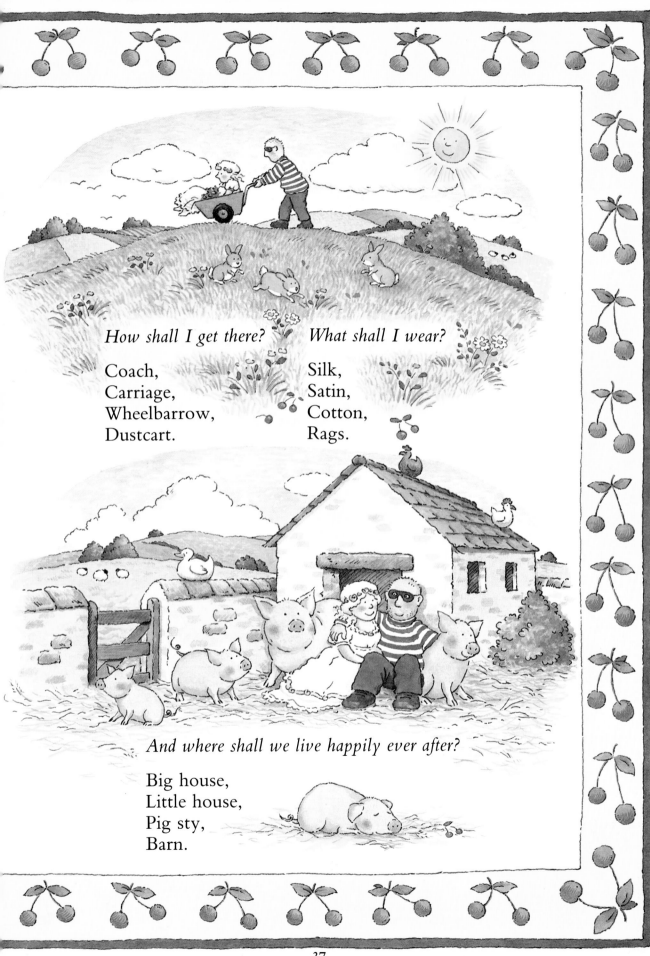

How shall I get there?   *What shall I wear?*

Coach,
Carriage,
Wheelbarrow,
Dustcart.

Silk,
Satin,
Cotton,
Rags.

And where shall we live happily ever after?

Big house,
Little house,
Pig sty,
Barn.

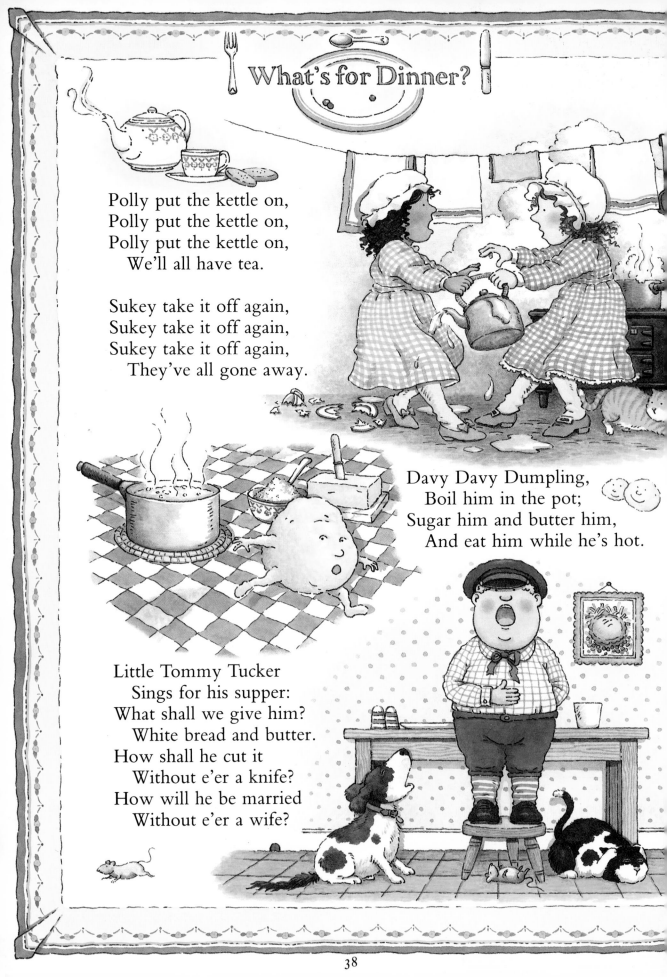

What's for Dinner?

Polly put the kettle on,
Polly put the kettle on,
Polly put the kettle on,
  We'll all have tea.

Sukey take it off again,
Sukey take it off again,
Sukey take it off again,
  They've all gone away.

Davy Davy Dumpling,
  Boil him in the pot;
Sugar him and butter him,
  And eat him while he's hot.

Little Tommy Tucker
  Sings for his supper:
What shall we give him?
  White bread and butter.
How shall he cut it
  Without e'er a knife?
How will he be married
  Without e'er a wife?

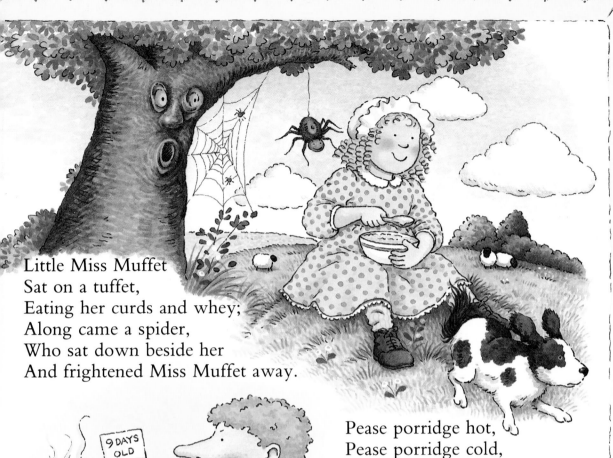

Little Miss Muffet
Sat on a tuffet,
Eating her curds and whey;
Along came a spider,
Who sat down beside her
And frightened Miss Muffet away.

Pease porridge hot,
Pease porridge cold,
Pease porridge in the pot
Nine days old.
Some like it hot,
Some like it cold,
Some like it in the pot
Nine days old.

9 DAYS OLD

Jack Sprat could eat no fat,
   His wife could eat no lean;
And so between them both, you see,
   They licked the platter clean.

Bad Boys and Naughty Girls

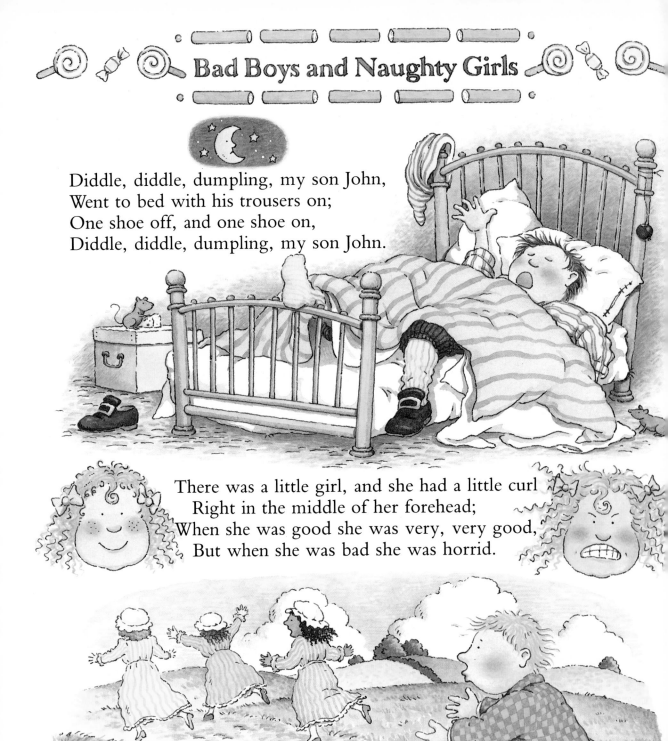

Diddle, diddle, dumpling, my son John,
Went to bed with his trousers on;
One shoe off, and one shoe on,
Diddle, diddle, dumpling, my son John.

There was a little girl, and she had a little curl
Right in the middle of her forehead;
When she was good she was very, very good,
But when she was bad she was horrid.

Georgie Porgie, pudding and pie,
Kissed the girls and made them cry;
When the boys came out to play,
Georgie Porgie ran away.

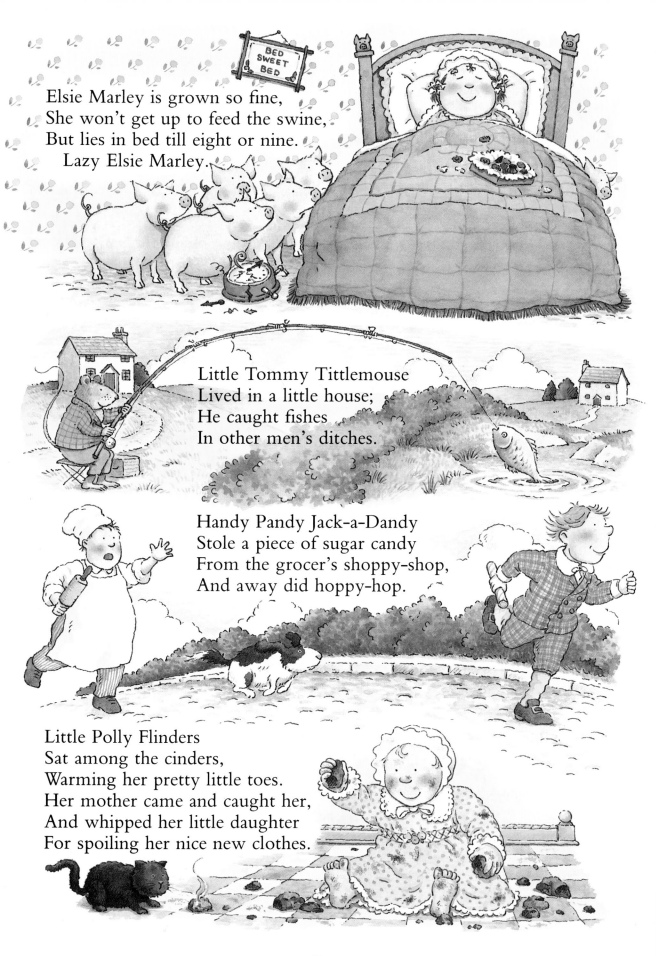

Elsie Marley is grown so fine,
She won't get up to feed the swine,
But lies in bed till eight or nine.
   Lazy Elsie Marley.

Little Tommy Tittlemouse
Lived in a little house;
He caught fishes
In other men's ditches.

Handy Pandy Jack-a-Dandy
Stole a piece of sugar candy
From the grocer's shoppy-shop,
And away did hoppy-hop.

Little Polly Flinders
Sat among the cinders,
Warming her pretty little toes.
Her mother came and caught her,
And whipped her little daughter
For spoiling her nice new clothes.

Jack and Jill

Jack and Jill
Went up the hill,
To fetch a pail of water;
Jack fell down,
And broke his crown,
And Jill came tumbling after.

Then up Jack got,
And home did trot,
As fast as he could caper;
He went to bed,
To mend his head,
With vinegar and brown paper.

Pigs to Market

To market, to market, to buy a fat pig,
Home again, home again, jiggety jig;
To market, to market, to buy a fat hog,
Home again, home again, jiggety jog.

Tom, Tom, the piper's son,
Stole a pig and away he run;
The pig was eat,
And Tom was beat,
And Tom went howling down the street.

Dickery, dickery, dare,
The pig flew up in the air;
The man in brown
Soon brought him down
Dickery, dickery, dare.

Higglety, pigglety, pop!
The dog has eaten the mop;
The pig's in a hurry,
The cat's in a flurry,
Higglety, pigglety, pop!

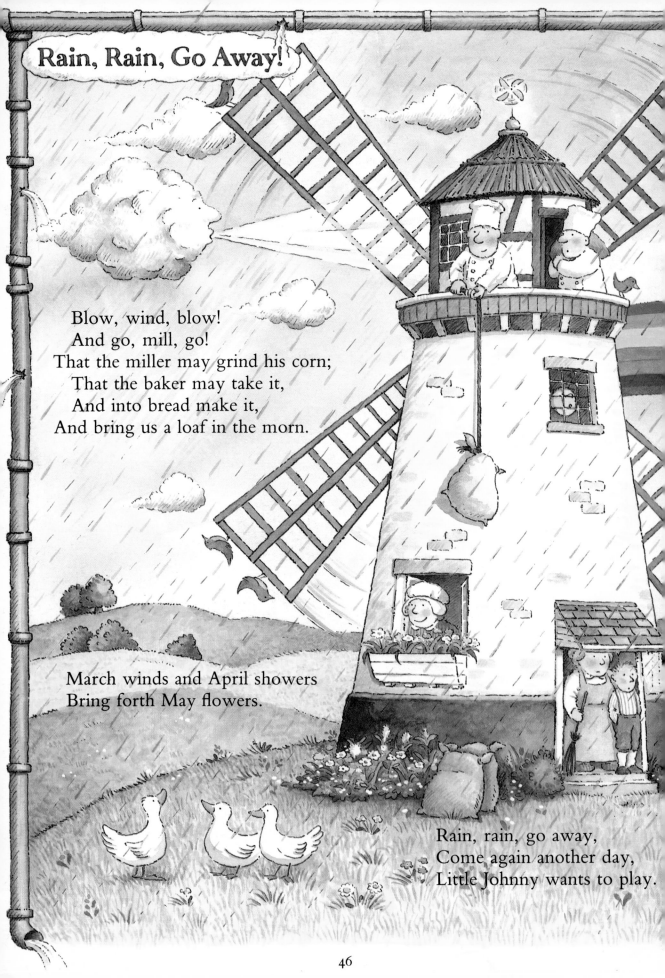

Rain, Rain, Go Away!

Blow, wind, blow!
And go, mill, go!
That the miller may grind his corn;
That the baker may take it,
And into bread make it,
And bring us a loaf in the morn.

March winds and April showers
Bring forth May flowers.

Rain, rain, go away,
Come again another day,
Little Johnny wants to play.

The Eency Weency spider
  Climbed up the waterspout;
Down came the rain
  And washed the spider out:
Out came the sun
  And dried up all the rain;
So the Eency Weency spider
  Climbed up the spout again.

A sunshiny shower
Won't last half an hour.

Rain on the green grass,
  And rain on the tree,
Rain on the housetop,
  But not on me.

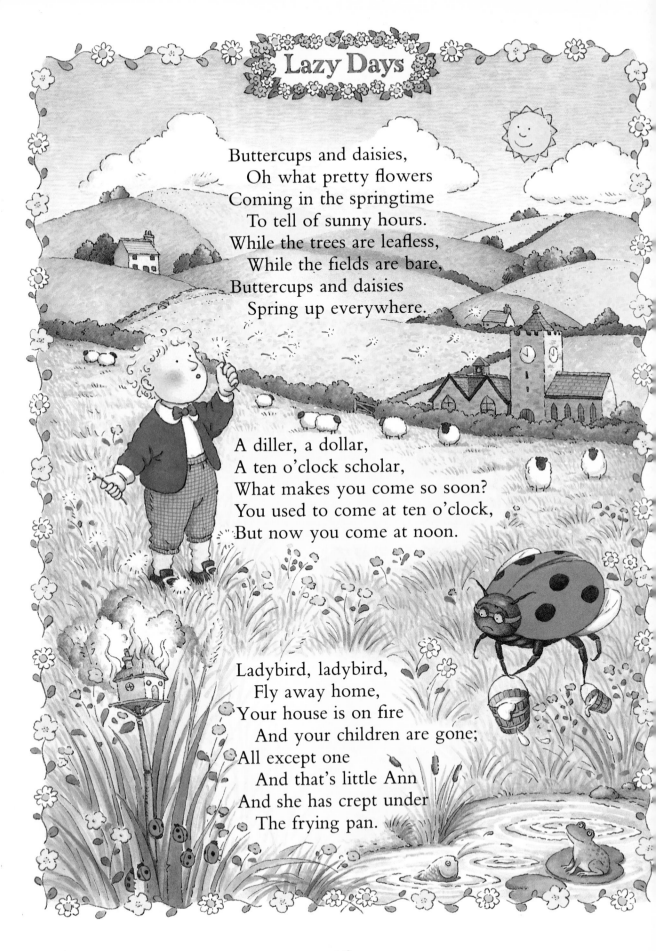

Lazy Days

Buttercups and daisies,
Oh what pretty flowers
Coming in the springtime
To tell of sunny hours.
While the trees are leafless,
While the fields are bare,
Buttercups and daisies
Spring up everywhere.

A diller, a dollar,
A ten o'clock scholar,
What makes you come so soon?
You used to come at ten o'clock,
But now you come at noon.

Ladybird, ladybird,
Fly away home,
Your house is on fire
And your children are gone;
All except one
And that's little Ann
And she has crept under
The frying pan.

The cock's on the woodpile
   Blowing his horn,
The bull's in the barn
   A-threshing the corn,
The maids in the meadow
   Are making the hay,
The ducks in the river
   Are swimming away.

A swarm of bees in May
Is worth a load of hay;
A swarm of bees in June
Is worth a silver spoon;
A swarm of bees in July
Is not worth a fly.

Little Boy Blue,
   Come blow your horn,
The sheep's in the meadow,
   The cow's in the corn.
Where is the boy
   Who looks after the sheep?
He's under a haystack
   Fast asleep.
Will you wake him?
   No, not I,
For if I do,
   He's sure to cry.

I'm the king of the castle,
Get down you dirty rascal.

I'll sing you a song,
Nine verses long,
    For a pin;
Three and three are six,
And three are nine;
You are a fool,
    And the pin is mine.

Bow, wow, wow,
Whose dog art thou?
Old Tom Tinker's dog
Bow, wow, wow.

Finders keepers,
Losers weepers.

Here am I,
Little Jumping Joan;
When nobody's with me
I'm all alone.

Lucy Locket lost her pocket,
Kitty Fisher found it;
Not a penny was there in it,
Only ribbon round it.

The Toy Cupboard

Little John Jiggy Jag,
He rode a penny nag,
    And went to Wigan to woo:
When he came to a beck,
He fell and broke his neck,
    Johnny, how dost thou now?

I made him a hat
Of my coat lap,
    And stockings of pearly blue;
A hat and a feather,
To keep out cold weather,
    So, Johnny, how dost thou now?

Jerry Hall,
He is so small,
A rat could eat him,
Hat and all.

I had a little moppet,
I kept her in my pocket
And fed her on corn and hay;
There came a proud beggar
And said he would wed her,
And stole my little moppet away.

Hush baby, my doll, I pray you don't cry,
And I'll give you some bread and some milk by and
    by;
Or, perhaps you like custard, or may be a tart,
Then to either you're welcome, with all my whole
    heart.

Work and Play

My maid Mary,
  She minds the dairy,
While I go a-hoeing and mowing
    each morn;
  Merrily she runs the reel,
  And the little spinning wheel,
While I am singing and mowing
    my corn.

Cobbler, cobbler, mend my shoe,
Get it done by half past two;
Stitch it up and stitch it down,
And I will you give you half a crown

Can you wash your father's shirt,
  Can you wash it clean?
Can you wash your father's shirt
  And bleach it on the green?
Yes, I can wash my father's shirt,
  And I can wash it clean.
I can wash my father's shirt
  And send it to the Queen.

Meadowsweet,
And thistledown,
Up the hill,
And tumble down.

There was a jolly miller once,
    Lived on the river Dee;
He worked and sang from morn till night,
    No lark so blithe as he.
And this the burden of his song
    Forever used to be,
I care for nobody – no! not I
    If nobody cares for me.

Wash the dishes, wipe the dishes,
    Ring the bell for tea;
Three good wishes, three good
        kisses,
    I will give to thee.

See-saw, Margery Daw,
Jacky shall have a new master;
Jacky shall have but a penny a day,
Because he can't work any faster.

Strange Folk

Goosey, goosey gander,
  Whither shall I wander?
Upstairs and downstairs
  And in my lady's chamber.
There I met an old man
  Who would not say his prayers,
I took him by the left leg
  And threw him down the stairs.

Peter, Peter, pumpkin eater,
Had a wife and couldn't keep her;
He put her in a pumpkin shell
And there he kept her very well.

Peter, Peter, pumpkin eater,
Had another, and didn't love her;
Peter learned to read and spell,
And then he loved her very well.

Mrs. Mason bought a basin,
Mrs. Tyson said, What a nice 'un,
What did it cost? said Mrs. Frost,
Half a crown, said Mrs. Brown,
Did it indeed? said Mrs. Reed,
It did for certain, said Mrs. Burton.
Then Mrs. Nix up to her tricks
Threw the basin on the bricks.

There was an old woman tossed up in a basket,
Seventeen times as high as the moon;
Where she was going I couldn't but ask it,
For in her hand she carried a broom.
Old woman, old woman, old woman, quoth I,
Where are you going to up so high?
To brush the cobwebs off the sky!
May I go with you? Aye, by-and-by.

There was a crooked man
    And he walked a crooked mile;
He found a crooked sixpence
    Against a crooked stile;
He bought a crooked cat
    Which caught a crooked mouse,
And they all lived together
    In a little crooked house.

Doctor Foster went to Gloucester
In a shower of rain;
He stepped in a puddle,
Right up to his middle,
And never went there again.

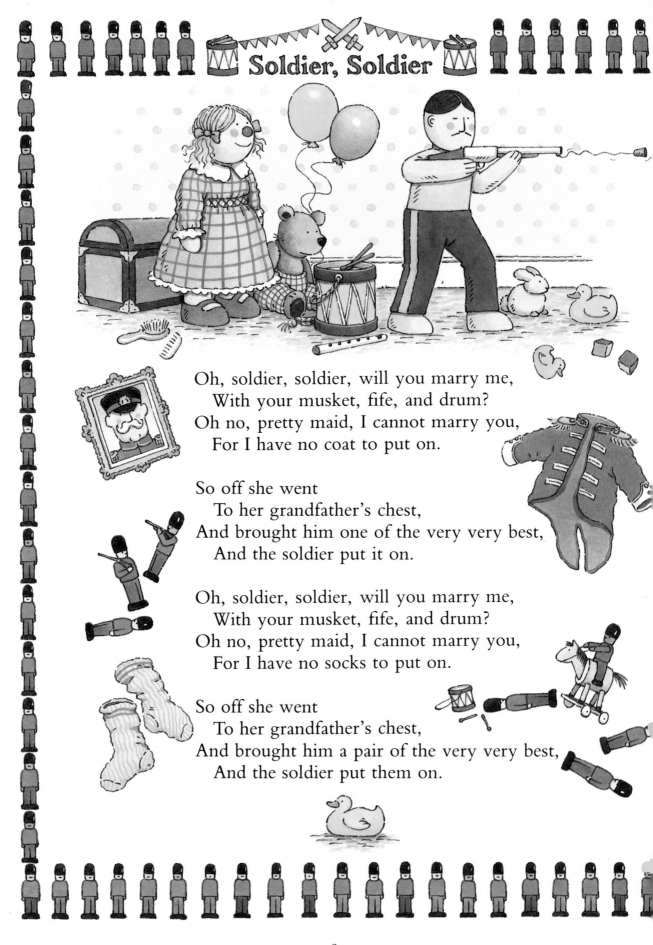

Soldier, Soldier

Oh, soldier, soldier, will you marry me,
 With your musket, fife, and drum?
Oh no, pretty maid, I cannot marry you,
 For I have no coat to put on.

So off she went
 To her grandfather's chest,
And brought him one of the very very best,
 And the soldier put it on.

Oh, soldier, soldier, will you marry me,
 With your musket, fife, and drum?
Oh no, pretty maid, I cannot marry you,
 For I have no socks to put on.

So off she went
 To her grandfather's chest,
And brought him a pair of the very very best,
 And the soldier put them on.

Oh, soldier, soldier, will you marry me,
   With your musket, fife, and drum?
Oh no, pretty maid, I cannot marry you
   For I have no shoes to put on.

So off she went
   To her grandfather's chest,
And brought him a pair of the very very best,
   And the soldier put them on.

Oh, soldier, soldier, will you marry me,
   With your musket, fife, and drum?
Oh no, pretty maid, I cannot marry you,
   For I have no hat to put on.

So off she went
   To her grandfather's chest,
And brought him one of the very very best,
   And the soldier put it on.

Oh, soldier, soldier, will you marry me,
   With your musket, fife, and drum?
Oh no, pretty maid, I cannot marry you,
   For I have a wife at home.

Fights and Fisticuffs

The lion and the unicorn
    Were fighting for the crown;
The lion beat the unicorn
    All around the town.

Some gave them white bread,
    And some gave them brown;
Some gave them plum cake
    And drummed them out of town.

Tweedledum and Tweedledee
    Agreed to have a battle,
For Tweedledum said Tweedledee
    Had spoiled his nice new rattle.
Just then flew by a monstrous crow
    As big as a tar barrel,
Which frightened both the heroes so,
    They quite forgot their quarrel.

Oh, the grand old Duke of York,
He had ten thousand men;
He marched them up
To the top of the hill,
And he marched them down again.

And when they were up, they were up,
And when they were down, they were down,
And when they were only halfway up,
They were neither up nor down.

Punch and Judy
    Fought for a pie;
Punch gave Judy
    A knock in the eye.
Says Punch to Judy,
    Will you have any more?
Says Judy to Punch,
    My eye is too sore.

Kings and Queens

Old King Cole
Was a merry old soul,
And a merry old soul was he;
 He called for his pipe,
 And he called for his bowl,
And he called for his fiddlers three.

Every fiddler he had a fiddle,
And a very fine fiddle had he;
 Oh, there's none so rare
 As can compare
With King Cole and his fiddlers
  three.

Hector Protector was dressed all in green;
Hector Protector was sent to the Queen.
  The Queen did not like him,
  No more did the King;
So Hector Protector was sent back again.

Lavender's blue, diddle, diddle,
Lavender's green;
When I am king, diddle, diddle,
You shall be queen.

I had a little nut tree,
Nothing would it bear
But a silver nutmeg
And a golden pear;
The king of Spain's daughter
Came to visit me,
And all for the sake
Of my little nut tree.
I skipped over water,
I danced over sea,
And all the birds in the air
Couldn't catch me.

The Queen of Hearts
She made some tarts,
All on a summer's day;
The Knave of Hearts
He stole those tarts,
And took them clean away.

The King of Hearts
Called for the tarts,
And beat the knave full sore;
The Knave of Hearts
Brought back the tarts,
And vowed he'd steal no more.

Bow-Wow Says the Dog

I had a dog
 Whose name was Buff,
I sent him for
 A bag of snuff;
He broke the bag
 And spilled the stuff,
And that was all
 My penny's worth.

Old Mother Hubbard
Went to the cupboard,
To fetch her poor dog a bone.
When she got there,
The cupboard was bare,
And so the poor dog had none.

I had a dog and his name was Dandy,
His tail was long and his legs were bandy,
His eyes were brown and his coat was sandy,
The best in the world was my dog Dandy.

Oh where, oh where has my little dog gone?
Oh where, oh where can he be?
With his ears cut short and his tail cut long,
Oh where, oh where is he?

Hark, hark,
   The dogs do bark,
The beggars are coming to town;
   Some in rags,
   And some in jags,
And one in a velvet gown.

All the Fun of the Fair

Smiling girls, rosy boys,
Come and buy my little toys;
Monkeys made of gingerbread,
And sugar horses painted red.

As I was going to Banbury,
   Upon a summer's day,
My dame had butter, eggs, and fruit,
   And I had corn and hay.
Joe drove the ox, and Tom the swine,
   Dick took the foal and mare;
I sold them all, then home to dine,
   From famous Banbury fair.

TICKETS

Hot cross buns! Hot cross buns!
One a penny, two a penny,
Hot cross buns!
If your daughters do not like them
Give them to your sons;
One a penny, two a penny,
Hot cross buns.

Gee-up, Neddy, to the fair,
What shall I buy when I get there?
A ha'penny apple, a penny pear.
Gee-up, Neddy, to the fair.

Oh Dear, What Can the Matter Be?

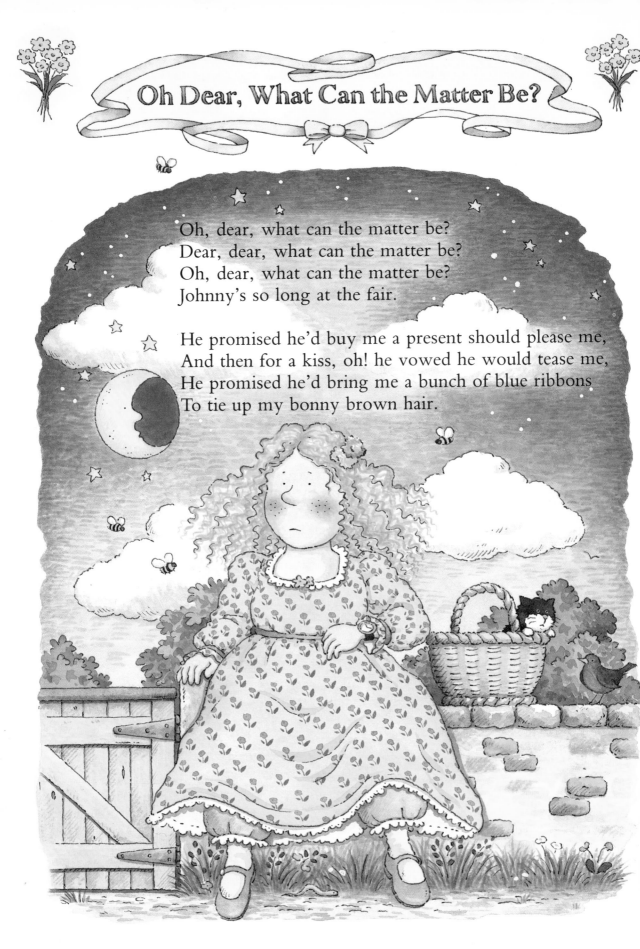

Oh, dear, what can the matter be?
Dear, dear, what can the matter be?
Oh, dear, what can the matter be?
Johnny's so long at the fair.

He promised he'd buy me a present should please me,
And then for a kiss, oh! he vowed he would tease me,
He promised he'd bring me a bunch of blue ribbons
To tie up my bonny brown hair.

Oh, dear, what can the matter be?
Dear, dear, what can the matter be?
Oh, dear, what can the matter be?
Johnny's so long at the fair.

He promised he'd bring me a basket of posies,
A garland of lilies, a garland of roses,
A little straw hat, to set off the blue ribbons
That tie up my bonny brown hair.

Oh, dear, what can the matter be?
Dear, dear, what can the matter be?
Oh, dear, what can the matter be?
Johnny's so long at the fair.

Join Hands!

Poor Mary lies a-weeping, a-weeping, a-weeping,
Poor Mary lies a-weeping, on a bright summer's day!

Oh, why is she a-weeping, a-weeping, a-weeping?
Oh, why is she a-weeping, on a bright summer's day?

She's weeping for her true love, her true love, her true love,
She's weeping for her true love, on a bright summer's day.

On the carpet she must kneel,
Till the grass grows in the field,
Stand up now, upon your feet,
Choose the one you love so sweet!

Now you're married we wish you joy,
First the girl, and then the boy.
Kiss her once, kiss her twice,
Kiss her three times over!

Ring around the rosy,
A pocket full of posies,
 A-tishoo! A-tishoo!
We all fall down.

The cows are in the meadow
Lying fast asleep,
 A-tishoo! A-tishoo!
We all get up again.

Little Love Ditties

Curly locks, Curly locks,
   Wilt thou be mine?
Thou shalt not wash dishes
   Nor yet feed the swine;
But sit on a cushion
   And sew a fine seam,
And feed upon strawberries,
   Sugar, and cream.

INGREDIENTS
IN

What are little boys made of?
What are little boys made of?
   Frogs and snails
   And puppy-dogs' tails,
That's what little boys are made of.

What are little girls made of, made of?
What are little girls made of?
   Sugar and spice
   And all things nice,
That's what little girls are made of.

OUT

OUT

BOY GIRL

One I love,
Two I love,
Three I love, I say,
Four I love with all my heart,
Five I cast away;
Six he loves me,
Seven he don't,
Eight we're lovers both;
Nine he comes,
Ten he tarries,
Eleven he courts,
Twelve he marries.

He loves me,
He don't,
He'll have me,
He won't
He would
If he could,
But he can't,
So he don't.

She loves me,
She loves me not,
She loves me,
She loves me not,
She loves me!

Roses are red,
Violets are blue,
Sugar is sweet
And so are you.

Are We Nearly There?

How many miles to Babylon?
Threescore and ten.
Can I get there by candlelight?
Yes, and back again.
If your heels are nimble and light,
You may get there by candlelight.

Seesaw, sacradown,
Which is the way to London town?
One foot up and the other foot down
That is the way to London town.

The man in the moon
Came down too soon,
And asked his way to Norwich;
He went by the south,
And burned his mouth
With sipping cold plum porridge.

Three wise men of Gotham
Went to sea in a bowl;
If the bowl had been stronger,
My tale would be longer.

Where Are You Going to, My Pretty Maid?

Where are you going to, my pretty maid?
I'm going a-milking, sir, she said,
Sir, she said, sir, she said,
I'm going a-milking, sir, she said.

May I go with you, my pretty maid?
You're kindly welcome, sir, she said,
Sir, she said, sir, she said,
You're kindly welcome, sir, she said.

Say, will you marry me, my pretty maid?
Yes, if you please, kind sir, she said,
Sir, she said, sir, she said,
Yes, if you please, kind sir, she said.

What is your father, my pretty maid?
My father's a farmer, sir, she said,
Sir, she said, sir, she said,
My father's a farmer, sir, she said.

What is your fortune, my pretty maid?
My face is my fortune, sir, she said,
Sir, she said, sir, she said,
My face is my fortune, sir, she said.

Then I can't marry you, my pretty maid.
Nobody asked you, sir, she said,
Sir, she said, sir, she said,
Nobody asked you, sir, she said.

Bobby Shaftoe

Bobby Shaftoe's gone to sea,
Silver buckles at his knee;
He'll come back and marry me,
Bonny Bobby Shaftoe.

Bobby Shaftoe's bright and fair,
Combing down his yellow hair;
He's my love for evermore,
Bonny Bobby Shaftoe.

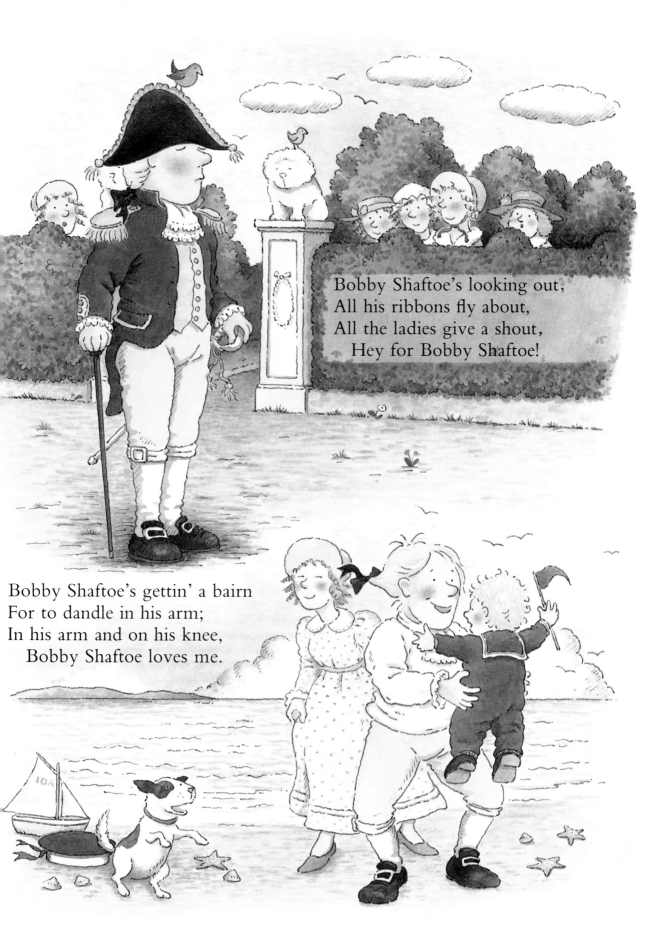

Bobby Shaftoe's looking out,
All his ribbons fly about,
All the ladies give a shout,
    Hey for Bobby Shaftoe!

Bobby Shaftoe's gettin' a bairn
For to dandle in his arm;
In his arm and on his knee,
    Bobby Shaftoe loves me.

Over Land and Sea

Over the water and over the lea,
  And over the water to Charlie.
I'll have none of your nasty beef,
  Nor I'll have none of your barley,
But I'll have some of your very best flour
  To make a white cake for my Charlie.

My mother sent me for some water,
For some water from the sea,
My foot slipped, and in I tumbled,
Three jolly sailors came to me:
One said he'd buy me silks and satins,
One said he'd buy me a golden ring,
One said he'd buy me a silver cradle
For to rock my baby in.

If all the world was paper,
    And all the sea was ink,
If all the trees were bread and cheese,
    What should we have to drink?

Little Tee Wee,
He went to sea
In an open boat:
And while afloat
The little boat bended,
And my story's ended.

If all the seas were one sea,
    What a great sea that would be!
If all the trees were one tree,
    What a great tree that would be!
And if all the axes were one axe,
    What a great axe that would be!
And if all the men were one man,
    What a great man that would be!
And if the great man took the great axe,
    And cut down the great tree,
And let it fall into the great sea,
    What a splish-splash *that* would be!

Here we go round the mulberry bush,
The mulberry bush, the mulberry bush,
Here we go round the mulberry bush,
On a cold and frosty morning.

This is the way we wash our hands,
Wash our hands, wash our hands,
This is the way we wash our hands,
On a cold and frosty morning.

This is the way we wash our clothes,
Wash our clothes, wash our clothes,
This is the way we wash our clothes,
On a cold and frosty morning.

This is the way we go to school,
Go to school, go to school,
This is the way we go to school,
On a cold and frosty morning.

This is the way we come out of school,
Come out of school, come out of school,
This is the way we come out of school,
On a cold and frosty morning.

Winter Songs

The north wind doth blow,
And we shall have snow,
And what will poor Robin do then?
    Poor thing.
He'll sit in a barn,
And keep himself warm,
And hide his head under his wing,
    Poor thing.

Cuckoo, cuckoo, cherry tree,
Catch a bird, and give it me;
Let the tree be high or low,
Let it hail or rain or snow.

Button to chin
When October comes in.
Cast not a clout
Till May be out.

Snow, snow faster,
Ally-ally-blaster;
The old woman's plucking her geese,
Selling the feathers a penny a piece.

Jingle bells! Jingle bells!
Jingle all the way:
Oh, what fun it is to ride
In a one-horse open sleigh!

Ring Out the Bells

Christmas is coming,
    The geese are getting fat,
Please put a penny
    In the old man's hat.
If you haven't got a penny,
    A ha'penny will do;
If you haven't got a ha'penny,
    Then God bless you!

Little Jack Horner
Sat in the corner,
Eating a Christmas pie;
He put in his thumb,
And pulled out a plum,
And said, What a good boy am I!

Merry are the bells, and merry would they ring,
Merry was myself, and merry could I sing;
With a merry ding-dong, happy, gay, and free,
And a merry sing-song, happy let us be.

God bless the master of this house,
    And its good mistress too,
And all the little children
    That round the table go;
And all your kin and kinsmen,
    That dwell both far and near;
We wish you a Merry Christmas
    And a Happy New Year.

Hush Little Baby

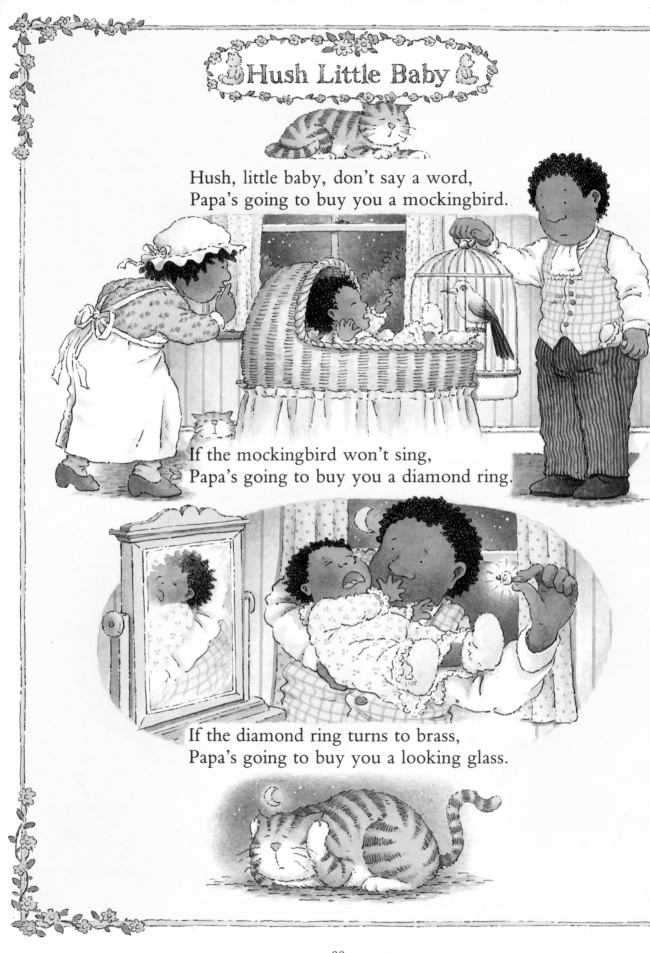

Hush, little baby, don't say a word,
Papa's going to buy you a mockingbird.

If the mockingbird won't sing,
Papa's going to buy you a diamond ring.

If the diamond ring turns to brass,
Papa's going to buy you a looking glass.

If the looking glass gets broke,
Papa's going to buy you a billy goat.

If that billy goat runs away,
Papa's going to buy you another today.

Boys and girls come out to play,
The moon doth shine as bright as day.
Leave your supper and leave your sleep,
And join your playfellows in the street.
Come with a whoop and come with a call,
Come with a good will or not at all.
Up the ladder and down the wall,
A halfpenny loaf will serve us all;
You find milk, and I'll find flour,
And we'll have a pudding in half an hour.

Jack be nimble,
  Jack be quick,
Jack jump over
  The candlestick.

Twinkle, twinkle, little star,
How I wonder what you are!
Up above the world so high,
Like a diamond in the sky.
Twinkle, twinkle, little star,
How I wonder what you are!

Wee Willie Winkie runs through the town,
Upstairs and downstairs in his nightgown,
Rapping at the window, crying through the lock,
Are all the children in their beds, it's now eight o'clock?

Good Night

Down with the lambs,
Up with the lark,
Run to bed children
Before it gets dark.

Good night, God bless you,
Go to bed and undress you.

Good night, sweet repose,
Half the bed and all the clothes.

Come, let's to bed,
Says Sleepyhead;
Tarry a while, says Slow;
Put on the pot,
Says Greedy-gut,
We'll sup before we go.

Rock-a-bye, baby,
  Thy cradle is green,
Father's a nobleman,
  Mother's a queen;
And Betty's a lady,
  And wears a gold ring;
And Johnny's a drummer,
  And drums for the king.

Go to bed first,
A golden purse;
Go to bed second,
A golden pheasant;
Go to bed third,
A golden bird.

INDEX OF FIRST LINES

E R

Rain, Rain, go away! : a boo
nur

Picture LANGLEY

Langley, Jonathan.

Rain, Rain, go away!